Tales From
Martha B. Rabbit

Written and Illustrated by
Shirley Barber

The Five Mile Press

The Five Mile Press Pty Ltd
950 Stud Road, Rowville
Victoria 3178 Australia
Email: publishing@fivemile.com.au
Website: www.fivemile.com.au

This edition first published 2002
Reprinted 2003, 2005
Originally published in three separate volumes

Stories and illustrations by Shirley Barber
Copyright © Marbit Pty Ltd
www.shirleybarbers.com
CD produced by Stephanie Mann, recorded at Spoken Word Productions

Printed in China

National Library of Australia
Cataloguing-in-Publication data
Barber, Shirley
Tales from Martha B. Rabbit

ISBN 1 86503 740 0

I. Rabbits - Juvenile fiction. I. Title.
A823.3

Contents

Small brown birds sing,
Nestlings on wing,
Gone is winter frost and snow.
Skies are deep blue,
And all day through,
Forest dwellers come and go.

Field mice scurry,
Rabbits hurry,
Each to work or market stall.
Then at day's end,
Homeward they wend;
Soon the evening shadows fall.

Come, on tip-toe,
Softly we'll go,
And through the tiny windows peep.
Wee hearths glow red,
Wee folk in bed,
All the forest is asleep.

Martha B. Rabbit and
The Unexpected Guests

Shirley Barber

Martha B. Rabbit and Tabitha cat stood at the
door of their apple-tree house and watched the
falling leaves.

"I never saw the autumn colours so bright," said
Tabitha, "nor so many nuts and berries in the forest!"

Martha looked anxious. "That often means a long,
cold winter is coming," she said. "We are going to
need plenty of firewood."

So they bought a load of firewood and stored it in the
shed. There it would stay dry for all their winter fires.

"And we will need to be warm at night," said
Martha. "Let's gather all the dried grass and stuff it
in our mattresses. That will keep us snug!"

Tabitha thought this was too much like hard work.
The hay seeds got in her dress and tickled her, and
the dust and dirt made her sneeze. Still, Martha was
nearly always right, so Tabitha worked hard to fill
her mattress, and all the spare ones, too.

"We'll put the left-over hay in the shed," said Martha
when they were finished. "Then we must tell every-
one in the forest to stock their cupboards with
enough food to last until spring."

So Tabitha and Martha organized a berry-picking and nut-gathering picnic.

The two robins who lived in the branches of the
apple-tree delivered their invitations.

Soon, cold winds blew all the autumn leaves from the trees leaving a tracery of bare branches against the wintry sky. The stream which flowed past the apple-tree house froze over, and each day Martha and Tabitha had to break a hole in the ice to draw water for their cooking.

"Look!" whispered Tabitha one frosty morning. "The deer have come to drink from the hole in the ice."

"Before long, they'll be coming to us for food," said Martha quietly. "There's not much left for them in the forest."

As the days went by it grew colder and colder, and then it began to snow. Soon it was so deep that Martha and Tabitha could walk no further than their own front steps.

That evening, an elf and two mice knocked on their door, weary and cold. They had been lost in the snow when they saw the lamplit windows of the apple-tree house, so had made their way towards it.

It was warm and cozy inside, and they all had fun playing games and reading to each other by the fire.

One bright but cold morning the deer came right up to the apple-tree house and asked for food, just as Martha said they would.

"There's hay in the shed," said Martha. "You can eat and sleep in there." But one little fawn was so weak that Martha let her stay inside by the fire.

The snowy weather continued, and soon the deer had eaten all the hay.

"What will they eat now?" whispered Tabitha.

"We'll take the hay from our mattresses and give them that," said Martha calmly. "We'll start with the spare beds, and hope the snow thaws before we have to take it from our own."

"Oh," said Tabitha. "Now I know why you made me fill our mattresses with hay."

Then one morning, when almost all the hay was finished, the sun broke through the winter clouds. The snow began to melt, and soon all the forest dripped and sparkled.

"Hooray!" laughed Tabitha. "The long, cold winter is coming to an end!"

The birds flew outside to perch in the apple-tree branches, and the mice scampered off to their homes. One by one, the deer bounded away as green grass shoots began to show through the melting snow.

"Goodbye," said the elf to Martha and Tabitha. "I promise to come back and visit you."

A few weeks later, the deer came back to thank
Martha and Tabitha for helping them through the
winter. Then they swept their friends up onto their
backs for a glorious ride through the forest.

And every spring after that, the fawn came back to
see them. One special year, her own little fawn came
with her.

The winters were never again quite so long and cold, but Martha and Tabitha always stored plenty of seeds, berries, nuts, and hay, just in case.

Tabitha still says to Martha, "Remember that winter we even had to take the hay out of our mattresses to feed the hungry deer?"

And Martha replies, "It certainly was a bad time — but we made a lot of very good friends, didn't we?"

Martha B. Rabbit and
Daphne the Forgetful Duck

Shirley Barber

One sunny morning, William Elf, Martha B. Rabbit and Tabitha Cat were busy working in their streamside garden.

Daphne paddled past them, on her way to market — with her six fluffy ducklings.

"Good morning!" she called to the three friends.

Next, the old herb woman rowed past in her little wooden boat. She was off to market to sell her bunches of sweet-smelling herbs.

"We must do our shopping, too," said Tabitha. So off to market they went.

When they arrived, the market was noisy and crowded. Right in the middle was Daphne, trying to keep her ducklings out of mischief.

Tabitha and Martha helped Daphne gather her ducklings together.

"Next time you go to market, leave your ducklings with us," said Martha to Daphne. "They can spend the morning at our apple-tree house."

"Oh, thank you," said Daphne. "That would be a great help."

So, the next market day, William, Tabitha and Martha waited all morning for Daphne and her ducklings — but they didn't come.

By lunchtime, the friends decided Daphne had forgotten.

"We can't wait any longer," said Martha, sighing. "We must do our own shopping before it gets too late."

They hurried off to market, and there, once again, they saw Daphne. She was quite frantic.

"I've lost my ducklings!" she sobbed. "I can't think where they are."

She had forgotten all about leaving them at the apple-tree house.

Tabitha and Martha did their best to calm Daphne down. They took her back to the apple-tree house, while William ran to fetch P.C. Tom.

"Where did you last see your ducklings?" P.C. Tom asked Daphne, but she simply couldn't remember.

"Perhaps they found their own way home," suggested William. "Tabitha and I will go and see."

So, while Daphne rested on the couch, William and Tabitha set off for Daphne's house at No. 1, Duck Pond Lane.

W illiam and Tabitha searched the garden for the ducklings, but could not find them.

"Look!" said William suddenly. "There's a note on the door."

Dear Mama -
We have gone to the meadow to play in the buttercups. We will be good like you told us and will be home by tea time
x x x x x x

"Daphne didn't take her ducklings to the market after all," he cried.

1
DUCK POND
LANE

"What a dreadful memory Daphne has," said Tabitha.

She and William hurried up the lane towards the meadow where they could see the ducklings playing. But they also saw two fox cubs, spying on the ducklings.

"What are those two cubs up to?" whispered Tabitha, as she and William hid in the bushes.

They heard the cubs talking about "tasty duckling pie" and "fetching Papa Fox and a bag" — the ducklings were in danger!

As the cubs ran off to fetch Papa Fox, Tabitha and William rounded up the ducklings and headed them towards the stream.

Luckily, just as they reached the stream, they saw the friendly herb woman from the market row by.

"Help!" Tabitha cried out to her. "The foxes are after the ducklings."

Soon, they were all safely in the herb woman's boat, rowing downstream towards the apple-tree house.

P.C. Tom called to them from the bank, glad to see the ducklings had been found. William told him what had happened, so he hurried away to catch the foxes in the meadow.

At last, the boat reached the apple-tree house.
How happy Daphne was to see her ducklings safe!

They told the old herb woman the whole story.

When it was finished, she said to Daphne, "The only reason you lost your ducklings is because your memory is so bad. Try my very special herbal tonic — it will soon make your memory much better."

And so it did! After that, Daphne always remembered to leave her ducklings at the apple-tree house on market morning. And the three friends went to market after lunch.

William and the ducklings became great friends, and Daphne never had to worry about her bad memory again.

Martha B. Rabbit and
Those Wicked Rats Again

Shirley Barber

One snowy winter's morning, in the house under the apple-tree, Martha B. Rabbit was in a hurry. Cuckoo hadn't woken her — as he usually did — so she was running late for work.

With a little help from Tabitha Cat, Martha was soon making her way to Mr. Gnome's Guesthouse. There, once a week, she cooked special food for Mr. Gnome to serve at the fairies' party — and today was the day.

"Why didn't you wake us this morning?"
Tabitha asked Cuckoo when Martha had gone.

Cuckoo looked sulky. "I won't wake you any more
unless you let me fly around the forest each
morning. I need fresh air and exercise!"

"All right," laughed Tabitha. "Why didn't you tell us
how you felt before?"

So, from that day on, Cuckoo always woke Martha
and Tabitha on time. Then, after breakfast, he
would fly into the forest. Later, he would bring
home all the forest news.

Not far from the apple-tree house lived three wicked rats, Blackie, Brownie and Spotto. One day, Cuckoo overheard them plotting to rob Martha on her way home from the fairies' party. Mr. Gnome always gave her a bag of food, and those wicked rats wanted it for themselves.

After Cuckoo told Tabitha what he'd heard, the pair went to spy on the rats. They saw them fill an umbrella with soft, fresh snow, then hang it upside-down from a tree.

The rats soon finished their work and went home to wait until dark. Once they were gone, Tabitha and Cuckoo hid in the tree.

When it grew dark, the rats returned — just in time to see Martha coming along the path. As she drew near, they hurried towards the tree.

But suddenly, Cuckoo fluttered towards them, cuckooing loudly.

"He'll give us away!" cried Blackie.

The rats ran out to chase Cuckoo away and — WHOOSH! Tabitha tipped the snow all over them!

A week later, Cuckoo brought home more bad news.

"Now those wicked rats have made a giant snowball," he told Tabitha. "Tonight, they're going to roll it onto Martha, then steal her food-bag as she falls."

"Oh dear," cried Tabitha. "I must do something to help Martha."

So, that evening, Tabitha hid near the huge snowball. Before long, the rats returned, laughing with glee at their new plan.

Soon the rats saw Martha's lantern gleaming in the distance, so they hurried towards the snowball. But, once again, Cuckoo flew towards them, cuckooing noisily.

All three rats ran to grab Cuckoo, but he quickly flew away. Tabitha came out from her hiding place and gave the huge snowball a mighty push.

Down the hill it rolled, gathering up Blackie, Brownie and Spotto as it went.

How surprised Martha was to see
a giant snowball full of rats!

The next week, Blackie announced yet another plan. Spotto and Brownie groaned, but at last agreed. Cuckoo heard the rats plotting, and spotted them pushing their sledge up the hill.

"Tonight," Cuckoo reported to Tabitha, "those wicked rats are going to sledge down the hill and snatch Martha's bag as they zoom by!"

"Oh no they won't," said Tabitha, putting on her coat.

She crept up the hill and found the sledge, then tied it to a tree with a long piece of rope.

That evening, when the rats saw Martha coming home, they pushed off their sledge as planned. They were half-way down the hill when . . .

...The sledge stopped— but the rats didn't!

They all went KER-SPLOSH into the ice-cold pond.

The rats crawled out of the pond.

"Why do you keep trying to rob me?" Martha asked the shivering rats.

"We've run out of food — and we're hungry," they replied through chattering teeth.

Martha didn't say anything. She just opened her bag and gave them a crusty loaf of bread, a whole cheese, and a big chocolate cake.

Later, Brownie and Spotto were very cross with Blackie.

"You got us into all that trouble for nothing," they said. "We only had to ask Martha nicely for some food!"

"I know," chuckled Blackie. "But that wouldn't have been nearly as exciting, would it?"